I Wish I Had a Pirate Suit

For Ben

VIKING
Published by the Penguin Group
Viking Penguin, a division of Penguin Books USA Inc.,
375 Hudson Street, New York, New York 10014, U.S.A.
Penguin Books Ltd, 27 Wrights Lane, London W8 5TZ, England
Penguin Books Australia Ltd, Ringwood, Victoria, Australia
Penguin Books Canada Ltd, 2801 John Street, Markham, Ontario, Canada L3R 1B4
Penguin Books (N.Z.) Ltd, 182–190 Wairau Road, Auckland 10, New Zealand

Penguin Books Ltd, Registered Offices: Harmondsworth, Middlesex, England

First published in Australia by Penguin Books Australia Ltd. 1989
First American edition published in 1990
1 3 5 7 9 10 8 6 4 2
Copyright © Pamela Allen, 1989
All rights reserved

LIBRARY OF CONGRESS CATALOGING IN PUBLICATION DATA
Allen, Pamela.   I wish I had a pirate suit / Pamela Allen.—1st American ed.   p.   cm.
Summary: Peter has a pirate suit and all the power to go with it,
while his younger brother has to serve as the crew on their
imaginary pirate ship.
ISBN 0-670-82475-5
[1. Brothers—Fiction. 2. Play—Fiction.] I. Title.
PZ7.A433Iaw 1990   [E]—dc20   90-70085

Printed in Hong Kong

I Wish I Had a Pirate Suit

Pamela Allen

VIKING

I wish I had a pirate suit.

Peter has a pirate suit
with ostrich feathers in his hat.
I wish I had one too.

Peter has a pirate suit.

He is the pirate captain
with a sword and pistol too.

Peter has a pirate suit.
He is the pirate captain
and I'm his only crew.

Peter has a pirate suit.
He's the captain of the pirate ship
and tells me what to do.

Peter has a pirate suit.
He is the boss of seven seas
and all their islands too.

Peter has a pirate suit.
He says that pirate captains
can cook you up for stew!

Peter has a pirate suit.
He says he's got a lot of gold,
and tons of treasure too.

Peter has a pirate suit.
He's eating all the jelly babies
and there's nothing I can do.

Peter has a pirate suit.
He's going to make me walk the plank
to feed a crocodile or two.

I wish I had a pirate suit,
Peter has a pirate suit.
He's got a pile of prisoners
and one of them is ME!

That was a long time ago
when I was only three.
Now I've grown bigger
and the pirate suit fits me.

Now I've got the pirate suit
although it's not quite new.
I could be the pirate captain
with a sword and pistol too.
I could be the pirate captain

but I haven't got a crew
because . . .

Now Peter is a lion tamer

and the lion is . . .

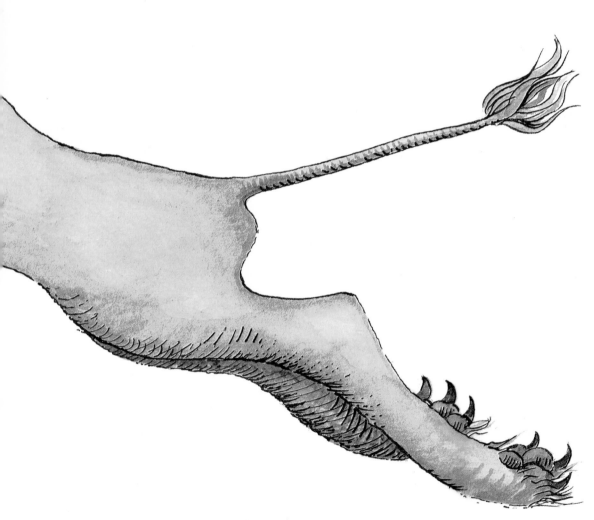

GUESS WHO?